FLIGHT OF THE QUETZALCOATLUS

OTHER BOOKS IN THE SERIES:

ATTACK of the **TYRANNOSAURUS**

CHARGE of the **TRICERATOPS**

MARCH of the **ANKYLOSAURUS**

CATCHING the **VELOCIRAPTOR**

STAMPEDE of the **EDMONTOSAURUS**

DINOSAUR COVE™

FLIGHT OF THE QUETZALCOATLUS

BY
X STONE

ILLUSTRATED BY
MIKE SPOOR

SCHOLASTIC INC.

New York Toronto London Auckland Sydney

Mexico City New Delhi Hong Kong Buenos Aires

SPECIAL THANKS TO JAN BURCHETT AND SARA VOGLER

ESPECIALLY FOR THEO AND BEN WHEADON, WITH LOVE

ISBN-13: 978-0-545-05380-8
ISBN-10: 0-545-05380-3

© 2008 by Working Partners Ltd. All rights reserved.
Illustrations © 2008 by Mike Spoor.

Dinosaur Cove series created by Working Partners Ltd., London. All rights reserved. Published by Scholastic Inc., 557 Broadway, New York, NY 10012, by arrangement with Working Partners Ltd. SCHOLASTIC, LITTLE APPLE, and associated logos are trademarks and/or registered trademarks of Scholastic Inc. DINOSAUR COVE is a registered trademark of Working Partners Ltd.

12 11 10 9 8 7 6 5 4 3 2 1   8 9 10 11 12 13/0

Printed in the U.S.A.
First printing, November 2008

FACT FILE

➡ JAMIE HAS JUST MOVED FROM THE CITY TO LIVE IN THE LIGHTHOUSE IN DINOSAUR COVE. JAMIE'S DAD IS OPENING A DINOSAUR MUSEUM ON THE BOTTOM FLOOR OF THE LIGHTHOUSE. WHEN JAMIE GOES HUNTING FOR FOSSILS HE MEETS A LOCAL BOY, TOM, AND THE TWO DISCOVER AN AMAZING SECRET: A WORLD WITH REAL, LIVE DINOSAURS! WALKING ON THE GROUND WITH THE DINOSAURS IS ONE THING, BUT FLYING IN THE AIR WITH THEM IS A DIFFERENT MATTER!

JAMIE

- FULL NAME: JAMIE MORGAN
- AGE: 8 YEARS
- SIZE: 1 JATOM*
- TOP SPEED: 7 MPH
- LIKES: FOSSIL HUNTING AND LEARNING ABOUT DINOSAURS
- DISLIKES: BEING STUCK INDOORS

Jamie's foot

Jamie's hand

*NOTE: A JATOM IS THE SIZE OF JAMIE OR TOM: 4 FT TALL AND 60 LB IN WEIGHT

TOM

- FULL NAME: THOMAS CLAY
- AGE: 8 YEARS
- SIZE: 1 JATOM*
- TOP SPEED: 7 MPH
- LIKES: TRACKING ANIMALS AND EXPLORING WILDLIFE
- DISLIKES: RAINY DAYS

Tom's eye   Tom's Hand

WANNA

- FULL NAME: WANNANOSAURUS
- AGE: 65 – 80 MILLION YEARS**
- SIZE: LESS THAN A JATOM*
- TOP SPEED: 30 MPH, ESPECIALLY WHEN BEING CHASED BY A T-REX
- LIKES: STINKY GINKGO FRUIT AND BANGING HIS HEAD ON TREE TRUNKS
- DISLIKES: SCARY DINOSAURS

Wanna's head   Wanna's foot

*NOTE: A JATOM IS THE SIZE OF JAMIE OR TOM: 4 FT TALL AND 60 LB IN WEIGHT
**NOTE: SCIENTISTS CALL THIS PERIOD THE LATE CRETACEOUS.

QUETZALCOATLUS

Quetzalcoatlus's claw

Quetzalcoatlus's eye

Quetzalcoatlus's beak

Quetzalcoatlus's talon

- **FULL NAME:** QUETZALCOATLUS
- **AGE:** 65 – 80 MILLION YEARS**
- **NECK:** LONGER THAN A GIRAFFE'S
- **WIDTH:** UP TO 14 JATOMS*
- **WEIGHT:** 5 JATOMS*
- **LIKES:** BEING THE LARGEST FLYING CREATURE EVER
- **DISLIKES:** BEING MISTAKEN FOR A DINOSAUR, IT WAS A PTEROSAUR, A FLYING LIZARD

*NOTE: A JATOM IS THE SIZE OF JAMIE OR TOM: 4 FT TALL AND 60 LB IN WEIGHT
**NOTE: SCIENTISTS CALL THIS PERIOD THE LATE CRETACEOUS

Landslips where
clay and fossils are

Muddy beach

DINO CAVE

tide beach line

w tide beach line

Sea

Smugglers' Point

"This exhibit looks so cool!" exclaimed Jamie, as his best friend Tom glued on the last miniature jungle tree.

The two boys had spent the morning painting the prehistoric landscape and were just finishing the scenery. The scale model was as big as the tabletop. It was going to be one of the exhibits in Jamie's dad's new dinosaur museum on the bottom floor of the old lighthouse where they lived.

"The marsh is my favorite," Tom said, putting down the glue.

The model was labeled "Late Cretaceous Period" and had a jungle, a plain, a beach with cliffs, and an eerie-looking marsh. Dad had set up a smoke machine under the table so that smoke blew over the marsh like mist.

Dad walked into the room with the newspaper. "You two have done a brilliant job painting the ocean," he told them, and grinned at their paint-splattered clothes. "And yourselves!"

Next, Jamie and Tom added the most important items to the display — the dinosaurs! They arranged a herd of triceratops on the green plain.

"They're just right there," said Dad. "They look as if they're grazing." He stuck his head into a crate and started rummaging. Sawdust flew everywhere. "Can't find the edmontosaurus," came his muffled voice. "I'm sure they're in here somewhere."

"Dad's models are great," whispered Jamie, "but they're not as good as the real thing."

Jamie and Tom had a secret. They had discovered the entrance to an amazing land of living dinosaurs, and they visited it whenever they could.

Jamie picked up a Tyrannosaurus Rex and made it run across the plain toward an ankylosaurus with a roar.

Tom snatched up the ankylosaurus. "Not such an easy meal, you bully!" He swung the tiny anky's clubbed tail at the T-Rex.

"Whoops!" Tom gasped as the T-Rex went flying out of Jamie's hand toward a shelf full of model creatures.

WHACK!

The T-Rex crashed into a large winged creature, which wobbled and fell. Jamie dived like a goalie and caught it before it hit the floor.

"Good catch!" gasped Tom.

Jamie's dad came running over.

"Sorry, Mr. Morgan," said Tom. "Is it broken?"

Jamie's dad checked the model's wings. "No damage done," he told them. "Now, where should this go in the display?"

Jamie looked at the long beak, the out-stretched wings, and bony crest on the head. "It's a type of pterosaur, isn't it?"

"Yes, it's a quetzalcoatlus. Here's its label."

"*Ket-sal-kow-at-lus*," Jamie read. "That's a mouthful."

"The biggest flying reptile of them all," Dad explained. "It had a forty-foot wingspan."

"That's more than six Dads lying head to toe." Jamie flung his arms out wide.

"What a monster!" Tom said.

"One thing we don't know

is where these quetzies nested," said Dad. "On the marsh, on the beach, or in the jungle?" He put the quetzy back on the shelf. "Here's a quest for you, boys. Do some research and help me decide where on the model to put it. That'll keep you out of trouble."

Jamie and Tom grinned at each other. They knew exactly how to find out where the quetzalcoatlus nested — in Dino World!

Jamie scooped up his backpack and charged after Tom down the rocky steps from the lighthouse. They raced across the pebbly beach, whooping with excitement, to the steep headland path. They clambered over the mossy boulders and were soon at the old smugglers' cave — and the entrance to their secret world.

Tom slipped inside with
Jamie close behind. They
squeezed through the tiny opening to the second chamber.
Jamie shone his flashlight over
the rock floor.

"Here are the footprints," he said. "Let's go!"

One step at a time, Jamie and Tom followed the fossilized dinosaur tracks that led to the wall at the back of the cave. One . . . two . . . The familiar crack of light appeared in the wall . . . three . . . four . . . The crack widened . . . five!

Suddenly, the ground was spongy under his feet. Jamie and Tom were in Dino World again!

CHAPTER 2

Jamie stepped out of the cave and squinted in the bright sunlight. He breathed in the hot, damp air. "Awesome!"

A bristly tongue licked his hand. A little dinosaur with greenish brown markings stood looking up hopefully at him.

"It's Wanna!" he cried.

Tom gave the wannanosaurus a welcoming pat on his hard, flat head. Wanna wagged his tail happily and stuck out his tongue to investigate a blue spot on Jamie's shorts.

Grunk! Wanna spat.

"Paint tastes horrible, doesn't it, Wanna?" said Jamie. "Let's find you some nice, stinky ginkgoes to make it better." He reached up and picked a handful of sticky orange fruits from a nearby ginkgo tree.

Wanna gulped down the ginkgoes in one big gulp, juice spilling out of his mouth and down his chest. His long, bristly tongue licked his face, and he grunted happily.

Jamie stuck a few more ginkgoes in his backpack.

The boys went to the edge of the steep slope that led down to the jungle. They scanned the thick green canopy of trees below.

"One thing's for sure," said Tom, "quetzies couldn't live in there — not with that huge wingspan. The trees are too close together. And I don't see any nests in the treetops."

Jamie opened his Fossil Finder and searched for quetzalcoatlus.

THOUGHT TO HAVE EATEN LIKE HERON, DIVING DOWN FOR FISH, he read.

"So maybe they live near water."

"Misty Lagoon?" said Tom. "But I only remember seeing smaller pterosaurs there — nothing as big as a quetzy."

"How about White Ocean?" said Jamie eagerly. He shielded his eyes with his hand and peered out over the jungle, to where the ocean waves broke in a white line.

Tom whipped his compass out of his pocket. "West it is."

The boys made their way down into the thick, damp undergrowth of the jungle. Wanna ran happily alongside them. He stopped to head butt a pine tree and greedily ate the cones that fell. The shower of cones disturbed a host of brightly colored butterflies as big as the boys' hands.

They swarmed for a moment and then settled on a bush covered in white flowers.

The boys crossed the river and gradually the dense jungle thinned. They passed the lagoon and the ground became sandy, with tall, spiky plants shooting up in places.

"I can hear waves breaking," exclaimed Tom. "Race you!"

They charged through the last few trees and out into the sunlight.

"Wow!" breathed Jamie, skidding to a halt. He pointed down the beach. "Check out those cliffs. They're even higher than back in Dinosaur Cove."

Sharp ledges and leafy green bushes covered the huge cliff face. In front of them, the golden beach stretched toward the water. Wanna sniffed around, getting his snout covered in sand.

"Maybe this is his first trip to the beach." Jamie laughed. "Sorry we forgot the bucket and shovel, Wanna."

"Awesome!" shouted Tom above the sound of the crashing breakers and the gusting wind. "Look at those waves. Fantastic for surfing."

"If you don't mind the predators," Jamie

reminded him. "I bet it's not just lobsters and crabs under there." He typed *LATE CRETACEOUS SEA CREATURES* into the Fossil Finder and scrolled down the entries. *ELASMOSAURUS: HUGE, LONG-NECKED, MARINE REPTILE.* "Looks like the

Loch Ness Monster."
He showed Tom the
picture on the screen.
PLATECARPUS: SHARP-TOOTHED
SEA LIZARD. "There are sharks, too."

"I could do a great TV commentary
from my surfboard." Tom pretended to be rid-
ing the waves and speaking into a microphone.
"Here we have the gigantic platecarpus. I can
see every one of this sea lizard's jagged teeth
and . . . *Aaaaagh*, it's got me!"

Jamie laughed as his friend fell on
the sand and fought an invisible
platecarpus.

Suddenly Tom jumped to his feet. "What's that?" He pointed to the horizon. "It's the size of a plane."

Jamie screened his eyes with his hand. Far away over the sea, a huge winged creature was gliding in large graceful circles, rising and falling with the air currents.

Tom whistled. "It's just like your dad's model. And look, here come some more."

The two boys looked at each other.

"It's a quetzalcoatlus!" they shouted.

CHAPTER 3

Jamie and Tom watched as the huge quetzies made lazy circles above the surf. One of them was getting closer.

"It's searching for fish," said Tom. "Do you think its nest is nearby?"

"It might be in the sand," suggested Jamie. "Like a turtle's."

They walked along the high-tide line, crunching through fragments of patterned baculite shell, but couldn't see any imprints or patterns in the ground to suggest a nest.

"Wouldn't this look good in your dad's museum?" Tom said, picking up a shell. "Too bad it would just turn to dust if we took it back."

"Even if we could," added Jamie, "these have been extinct for millions of years. Dad would want to know how we found one that's not a fossil."

Wanna trotted down the beach and looked suspiciously at the waves.

"Going for a paddle, Wanna?" called Tom.

The little dinosaur crept toward the edge of the water and stuck his snout into the surf.

Grunk!

He spluttered and darted back. The boys burst out laughing.

 22

"The salt must taste worse than paint," said Jamie. "Poor Wanna."

Wanna scratched at his mouth with his front claws as if he was trying to get rid of the taste.

Then Tom spotted a cave at the bottom of the cliffs. "That would be a great hiding place for the quetzy's nest."

The boys went to investigate. Jamie pulled out his flashlight and shone it into the dark beyond the cave entrance. It was empty. There was no sign of a quetzy nest.

AAARK!

The boys whirled around at the deafening

sound behind them. An enormous shadow was moving over the sand. They dived into the cave mouth. Wanna grunked in alarm and followed.

A gigantic creature swept down and landed on the sand with a loud flapping of wings that sounded like boat sails in the wind. Jamie and Tom stared in amazement. In front of them were two long, scaly legs with massive clawed feet. They looked up to see a featherless body that seemed to snake up to the sky. It stood above them, as tall as a house, twisting its long neck slowly this way and that. Then it opened its beak and gave out a loud *AAARK!*

"It's the quetzy," breathed Tom.

"That's one weird reptile," said Jamie in amazement. "Like a fold-up paper airplane with skin for wings."

The huge pterosaur began to clump awkwardly across the sand, head forward, using the claws on its wings as front feet.

"Bats walk like that," said Tom. "I've seen it on a wildlife program."

A gust of wind buffeted the quetzy. It ran a few steps on its long skinny legs, caught the updraft, and took off.

"See where it goes!" cried Jamie.

The boys dashed out from the shelter of the cave mouth and watched the quetzalcoatlus rise. The wind sent it back toward the cliffs, but soon it turned and soared, flapping its powerful wings to gain height. It circled around the cliff top and descended, feet out for landing. At last, with a loud *AAARK*, it disappeared from view.

"I bet its nest is up *there*," said Jamie. "We have to get to the top."

"It'll be a tough climb," said Tom, squinting up at the cliff face. "But we can do it. There are indents for our feet."

"And we can use the bushes to cling to," agreed Jamie.

SQUAWK!

Something landed on the sand behind them. It lay on its back with its skinny feet in the air. It looked like a large, featherless chicken.

"Where did that come from?" exclaimed Tom, staring up at the cliffs.

"I don't know," gasped Jamie. "Watch out!"

They darted back as a second one fell out of the sky and plopped down onto the sand. "They must be coming from up there," Tom said.

A third creature appeared over the top of the cliffs. It flapped its wings desperately and then cartwheeled down, squawking, to land right in front of them.

"They've got crests." Tom pointed to the little bony lump on top of each head. "Long beaks, claws on their wings . . ."

"They're baby quetzies!"

The boys watched as the three young reptiles struggled to their feet and waddled up and down, flapping their wings.

"They're trying to take off," said Tom.

"They look like big windup toys." Jamie grinned at the funny sight.

Grunk, grunk!

Wanna scuttled up to the gawky creatures. The baby quetzies peered down at him and squawked happily. "What is it, boy?" asked Jamie. "Are you saying hello?"

Grunk!

Wanna nudged the nearest chick with his nose, then darted out of reach. The little quetzies clumped after him on all fours, squeaking with delight. Wanna stopped, waggled his tail at them, and dashed off down the beach. His new playmates followed.

Tom chuckled. "They're playing tag. Let's get a closer look."

As soon as they saw the boys coming, the baby quetzies left Wanna and waddled toward them.

"They're not scared of us," said Tom. "They look really friendly."

"Whoa!" Jamie backed off as a long, pointed beak was pushed in his face, and another pecked at his sneakers. "A bit too friendly."

AAARK! The boys looked up. The mother quetzy was gliding in circles, looking down angrily, blocking out the sun.

"Run!" shouted Jamie.

Jamie and Tom flattened themselves against the cliff face, but Wanna hadn't noticed the danger. He ran around the babies, grunking and nudging them to play again.

"Wanna's in danger," said Tom. "The mother might attack him!"

"Come here, Wanna," Jamie shouted, but the little quetzies were making so much noise that Wanna didn't hear him.

AAARK!

The huge quetzalcoatlus began to descend, stretching out long, sharp claws as she came.

"We've got to save Wanna!" yelled Jamie, darting forward.

"It's too late." Tom pulled his friend back. "There's nothing we can do."

Swoosh! The boys felt the rush of air as the giant pterosaur swooped down over the sand. A second later she was making for the sky.

The babies were gone — and so was Wanna!

CHAPTER 4

Jamie and Tom stared openmouthed as the quetzalcoatlus rose in the air. Wanna and the three chicks were dangling from her claws. They could see the little dinosaur's tail waggling with fright.

Jamie shook Tom's arm. "We've got to get up those cliffs," he urged. "We must rescue Wanna."

"You're right," said Tom. "Before he's turned into quetzy food!"

They began to climb, side by side. It was a

slow job. The cliff footholds were very small, and the pale rock crumbled under their sneakers. Gradually they edged their way up.

"What's that?" Jamie asked, looking at something jutting out above them.

"Looks like a ledge of rock," Tom said. "It sticks out quite far. And we've got to get over it."

Luckily the ledge was covered in vines.

Jamie gave one a tug. It held firm. "There's only one way to go," he said.

"Okay, boss." Tom grinned.

Gripping tightly with his hands and hooking his feet over the vines, Jamie hung upside down underneath the ledge. He made his way like a spider on a ceiling to the edge of the overhang. He scrabbled with his fingers to find a handhold on the top of the ledge.

Suddenly he lost his grip and found himself hanging by his sneakers. It was like dangling from a giant jungle gym — a jungle gym with a deadly drop beneath it.

"Jamie!" yelled Tom in alarm.

"I'm okay," Jamie shouted back. He swung his arms up as hard as he could and on the third attempt managed to grab the foliage again. He waited until he'd gotten his breath back, then, tensing every muscle, he heaved himself onto the top of the ledge.

Soon Tom's hand appeared. Jamie took him

firmly by the wrist and helped him up. The boys saw that the top of the ledge was also covered by a spongy bed of vines.

"Awesome!" breathed Tom. "We did it."

"And there's the top of the cliffs," cried Jamie, pointing a little way above their heads. "Wanna, here we come!"

They scrambled up to the cliff edge and looked over. It was nothing like the cliffs back home, which were covered in grass and wildflowers. Here there was bare rock with a few scattered prickly plants sticking up. The mother quetzy sat a little way from them.

"There's no sign of Wanna," said Jamie, "or the babies."

"Let's get behind that bush with the red flowers," whispered Tom. "The quetzy won't be able to see us there."

Jamie and Tom crawled flat on their stomachs to the thick bush. Jamie carefully parted some leaves. The mother quetzy filled his view.

"The nest must be somewhere close by," he told Tom. "But it's hard to spot it with that huge pterosaur in the way."

"Ask her to move." Tom grinned.

"*You* ask her!"

As if she had heard, the mother quetzy waddled to the cliff edge, folded her wings, and raised her head, gazing out to sea.

"Look at the three bony crests over there," whispered Jamie. "Those are the babies. The mother must be guarding them in their nest."

The baby quetzies were sitting in a shallow hole a few yards away.

"But where's Wanna?" Tom grabbed Jamie's arm. "What if we're too late and they've already had him for dinner?"

Grunk, grunk!

A cone-shaped leathery hat with two brown eyes under it appeared over the edge of the nest.

"There he is!" exclaimed Tom.

"He's OK," breathed Jamie in relief. "But what's he wearing?"

"It's one of the quetzy eggshells." Tom giggled. He stuck a hand out of the bush. "Here, Wanna," he beckoned.

"Come on, Wanna," Jamie tried to coax him.

But Wanna just stared at them. He seemed comfortable with his new friends.

"How do we lure him out?" asked Tom.

Jamie rummaged in his backpack. "I'll offer him a ginkgo. That should bring him running."

Trying to keep out of sight of the mother, Jamie crawled toward the nest. He had reached the edge when she spotted him.

AAARK!

Jamie ducked as the huge wing nearly caught him. He darted back to the bushes and Tom pulled him between the leaves and out of sight. The ginkgo was squashed in his hand.

"It's just like on the documentaries," said Tom. "The mother is protecting her young, and that makes her very dangerous."

"One whack and I'd have been over the edge," puffed Jamie. "Now what?"

Tom didn't answer. He was looking up. Another quetzy was circling the nest.

"That one's even bigger than this one," he said. "It could be the dad."

AAARK, AAARK!

The male quetzy landed next to the nest. His cry was deep and rumbling. The babies greeted him with screeches and squeals. Their heads bobbed, and they eagerly opened their beaks. Wanna sat looking puzzled under his leathery hat. The dad bent his head down in a sudden motion and opened his mouth wide — right over Wanna's head. The boys heard a strange gurgling noise from his throat.

"He's going to eat him!" Jamie gasped. "We've got to do something."

But the male quetzy moved his head away from Wanna and over one of his babies. He made the strange gurgling sound again and threw up right into the baby quetzy's open

beak. The little chick gulped it down. Then the dad bent to the next chick and puked again. The chick opened its mouth, caught the goo, and ate hungrily.

"Gross!" said Jamie.

"It's just like birds feeding their young," said Tom. "They mash down the food in their own throats and then bring it back up for them. And it's Wanna's turn now."

The father gurgled again and all at once Wanna and his eggshell hat were covered in steaming yellow goo. Wanna looked surprised.

Jamie laughed. "They think he's one of their chicks!"

CHAPTER 5

Wanna shook his head, splattering yellow goo everywhere. His eggshell hat went flying. Then he clambered out of the nest and began to sniff and scuff at the ground.

"That's our Wanna," whispered Tom. "He never sits still for long. He's too nosy."

"I'd get out if a dinosaur threw up on my head," said Jamie.

Tom craned around the bush. "Wanna," he called softly. "Here, boy."

AAARK!

The mother quetzy had seen Wanna. Wriggling her wings irritably, she scuttled around the nest and nudged him back with her beak.

When the father had finished feeding all the chicks, he took off and soared away.

"This is our best chance to get Wanna," said Jamie. "I'd rather face one fierce quetzy than two."

"Agreed." Tom nodded.

The chicks began to squawk excitedly as the mother picked up one of them in her beak and plonked it down at the cliff edge.

"What's she doing?" Jamie gasped. "The baby's going to fall off again."

The little quetzy teetered on the edge for a moment and suddenly leaped off. They just had time to see it flapping its wings frantically before it plummeted out of sight.

The mother didn't seem to mind. She nudged another chick out of the nest and pushed it to the drop. This one flapped its wings and actually flew for a few seconds before it plunged down. They could hear its happy squawks as it fell.

"Of course," said Jamie. "It's Quetzy Flying School. The mom's teaching them how to fly."

"And the cliffs are a perfect launching site," said Tom. "Plenty of height."

The third baby waddled to the edge, opened its wings wide, and vanished from sight. The boys heard a squeal of triumph, and the little quetzy reappeared, flapping its wings and squawking at its mother. The mother quetzy squawked back encouragingly. Then the baby flew in a large circle and headed out to sea.

"Perhaps the mother will go off after them, and we can rescue Wanna," said Tom hopefully.

But now the mother quetzy was nudging Wanna toward the edge.

Jamie looked from Wanna to the cliff top. "She wants him to fly, too!"

"Uh-oh," Tom said. "We've got to save him!"

They darted out from their hiding place. Wanna was squatting on the edge of the cliff.

He grunked and flapped his front legs as if he had been watching the others.

AAARK! The mother quetzy was getting impatient. She prodded Wanna, and he nearly fell off the cliff.

Suddenly Jamie knew what to do.

"Grab him!" he yelled to Tom. "We'll all jump down and aim for the ledge below. It's our only chance."

Dodging under the mother quetzy's wings, the boys charged at Wanna, seized him around the middle, and leaped off the cliff.

Crunch!

They landed in a heap in the bouncy vines. One of the babies was there and it squealed with delight when it saw Wanna appear in front of him. The boys gave each other a high five.

"We made it!"

AAARK!

"It's the mom," said Jamie urgently, looking up.

The quetzy was peering over the edge of the cliff. She poked her long beak down, and the boys had to roll out of the way. She opened her wings and took to the air. "We'd better get out of here before she circles around to rescue her chick — and Wanna. But how are we going to get him to the beach?"

"Perhaps we can make a rope out of vines," suggested Tom. "Then we can lower him."

"It could work as long as we tie good knots," said Jamie.

Grunk, grunk!

They turned to see Wanna clambering to the far end of the ledge and disappearing from view.

"Wait, Wanna," cried Tom, scrambling across to see where he'd gone. "You'll fall!"

But to his surprise Wanna was trotting happily across the cliff face. He'd found a little trail that wound right down to the sand. The boys followed, placing each foot carefully on the narrow path.

"This is easier than the climb up," said Tom.

"But not as exciting," replied Jamie.

Swoosh! The mother quetzy swooped up past them, claws outstretched.

"She's come for her baby," said Tom. "I hope."

The quetzy glided gracefully to the ledge and

soon had her chick in her grasp. She made a wide, slow circle over the beach. The boys held their breath.

Was she coming for Wanna now?

But after an anxious moment she rose to the cliff top and disappeared.

As soon as the boys stepped onto the sand, Wanna bounded up and head butted them affectionately.

"Let's get you home, boy," said Tom. "Before your new mother comes looking for you."

They set off back into the jungle, Wanna running alongside them, grunting happily.

As they followed the river back to Wanna's cave, Jamie stopped and wrinkled his nose. "What's that smell?"

"It's Wanna," Tom laughed. "He's still covered in quetzy puke."

"Yuck!" Jamie held his nose. "Someone needs a bath."

He waded into the shallow water and held out a ginkgo. Wanna bounded into the river.

"Great," said Tom, jumping in to join them. "We can give him a shower."

He cupped his hands in the water and splashed Wanna all over.

Then Wanna turned and thumped the surface with his tail. Jamie and Tom got soaked.

"Thanks, Wanna," said Tom. "At least that gross yellow puke is gone."

Finally, they climbed out of the shadows and made their way up the hill to Wanna's cave.

Grunk.

Wanna ran straight to his nest and curled up.

"You've got the right nest this time." Jamie grinned. He took the last ginkgoes out of his bag and put them by Wanna's side. "See you soon, little friend."

They put their feet in the dinosaur footprints and walked backward toward the cave wall into the smugglers' cave. They hurried out of the cave and down the headland, running all the way along the beach to the path that led up Sealight Head. After waiting a little while for the sun to dry out their clothes, they raced up the steps, two at a time, and burst through the door of the lighthouse.

"We must have been away ages," gasped Jamie. "Dad's done so much."

They gazed at the breathtaking displays of dinosaur models and fossils all around the room.

"Awesome!" Tom pointed at a huge ammonite. "It's as big as a tire."

Jamie wandered around, taking it all in. "The triceratops skull looks great up on the wall."

His dad came in at that moment, laden with books.

"Hello there, boys," he called. "Found anything out about the quetzy nest?"

The boys went over to the model Cretaceous landscape. "We think it would have nested here on the cliff top," said Jamie. "There's lots of room for those huge wings, and it's a perfect takeoff point."

"The babies could learn to fly from there," added Tom eagerly. "It's very high and there'd be uplift from the wind coming off the ocean."

"Good thinking, boys," said Jamie's dad. He placed the quetzalcoatlus carefully down on the cliff top. "They'd be able to skim down over the sea and catch their dinner."

Jamie looked at the quetzalcoatlus model, its wings outstretched ready for flight. He winked at Tom.

"That's not all they catch," he whispered.

GLOSSARY

Baculite — an extinct sea creature that swam upside down with its head sticking out from the bottom of its long, thin shell. Because baculite fossils are fragile, fossil hunters rarely find a fossilized baculite shell intact.

Elasmosaurus — a long-necked prehistoric sea creature with a small head, sharp teeth, and four flippers. Elasmosaurus may have stretched 46 feet long, with its neck making up half of its total length.

Ginkgo — a tree native to China called a "living fossil" because fossils of it have been found dating back millions of years, yet they are still around today. Also known as the stink-bomb tree because of its smelly apricot-like fruit.

Platecarpus — an extinct sharp-toothed lizard with a long, flat tail and flippers. It may have swum like a snake in prehistoric waters.

Pterosaur — a prehistoric flying reptile. Its wings were leathery and light, and some of these "winged lizards" had fur on their bodies and bony crests on their heads.

Quetzalcoatlus — one of the largest flying animals ever. Named after the Aztec feathered serpent god Quetzalcoatl, this prehistoric bird had a long neck, toothless jaw, and a long, bony crest on top of its head. Its clawed wings could span up to 40 feet across.

Wannanosaurus — a dinosaur that only ate plants and used its hard, flat skull to defend itself. Named after the place it was discovered: Wannano, in China.